W9-DGW-423

MOUSE GETS CAUGHT

Roger Hargreaves

Publishers • GROSSET & DUNLAP • New York

Library of Congress Catalog Card Number: 81-84545
ISBN: 0-448-12316-9

First published in Great Britain by Hodder and Stoughton.
Published in the United States by Ottenheimer Publishers, Inc.
Published simultaneously in Canada.

MOUSE GETS CAUGHT

Exactly nine hundred and ninety-nine miles from where you're sitting now, stands Christmas Cottage.
And you know who lives in Christmas Cottage, don't you?
Hippo, Potto, and Mouse!

One evening, after young Mouse had gone to bed, Hippo and Potto sat in the living room complaining about him.

He's getting worse and worse," complained Potto.
He certainly isn't getting any better," agreed Hippo.
Why, do you know what he did to me the other day?"
What was that?" asked Potto.

Hippo had been getting ready to go to work one morning. As he was about to leave, Mouse handed him his umbrella and said, "You'd better take this, Hipp
It looks like rain."
"Thank you, Mouse," Hippo had said, and set off carrying his briefcase and umbrella.

Sure enough, halfway to the office, Hippo felt the first drops of rain.

"Mouse was right," thought Hippo to himself and opened his umbrella. But Mouse had filled Hippo's umbrella with flour!

White flour.

Poor Hippo!

Naughty Mouse!

"Oh, that's nothing," said Potto, "compared to what he did to me!" Potto had bought a rather smart new bowler hat, and Mouse had asked if he could put it on for him.

"That's most kind," Potto said. He bent down, and Mouse put the hat on his head. And off Potto had gone to Town.

But while he was walking through the Town, people had started pointing at his hat. At first, Potto had been rather pleased. But then he noticed that people were laughing at him.

And do you know what that naughty Mouse had done? He'd painted a face on Potto's hat. A funny face!

Poor Potto!

Naughty Mouse!

The following morning, Hippo was hanging clean clothes out to dry in the garden at Christmas Cottage. Do you know what Mouse did? He crept, quiet as the mouse he was, up behind the tree where the clothesline was tied. He had a grin on his face and a pair of scissors in his hand. And, just as Hippo finished—SNIP!

All the clean clothes fell in a muddy heap on the ground. And Hippo had to wash them all over again.
"Tee-hee-hee," giggled Mouse from behind the tree where he was hiding. "Tee-hee-hee!"
Hippo was not amused.

Later Potto got out of bed and came downstairs and sat down and ate the breakfast Hippo had left for him. When he got up, do you know what Mouse had done?

He'd spread honey on
Potto's kitchen stool!
Sticky honey!
And when Potto
stood up, the stool
stood up with him.
"Tee-hee-hee,"
giggled Mouse from
behind the door
where he was hiding.
"Tee-hee-hee!"
Potto was not amused.

That evening, again after Mouse had gone to bed, Hippo and Potto had another talk.
"Mouse needs to be taught a lesson!" said Potto indignantly.
"He needs a taste of his own medicine," agreed Hippo.
A small smile spread across Potto's face.
"A taste of his own medicine," he repeated. "Hippo, you have given me an idea!"
And he told him what the idea was.

The next day, when Mouse
came home from school
he looked in the kitchen.
And there, on the kitchen
table, stood a jar and a
bottle. And on the jar it
said HONEY in big letters.
And on the bottle it said
LEMONADE in big letters.
Mouse licked his lips.

"Mmm," said Mouse as he spread the honey nice and thick on a slice of bread.

"Mmm," said Mouse as he poured himself a large glass of bubbly lemonade.

"Mmm," said Mouse as he took a large bite of his honey sandwich.

"UGH!" sputtered Mouse as he tasted his honey sandwich. "UGH! OOO! UGH!"

As you have probably guessed, the honey sandwich wasn't a honey sandwich at all.
Do you know what it was?
A castor oil sandwich!
Potto had filled the honey jar with castor oil!

The taste was so horrible that Mouse grabbed the glass of lemonade and drank it all down at once to take that awful taste away.

"UGH!" sputtered Mouse again.

"UGH! OOO! UGH!"

As you have probably also
guessed, the lemonade wasn't
lemonade at all.
Do you know what it was?
The water that Hippo had use
for washing the clothes in!

Soapy water!
Hippo had filled the lemonade bottle full of soapy water!

Have you ever tried a castor oil sandwich, washed down with a large glass of soapy water? It does not taste nice. In fact, it tastes quite the opposite!
And you know what the opposite of nice is, don't you? Nasty!

But it taught Mouse his lesson, and he hasn't tried any more tricks on Hippo and Potto.

And that is the end of the story about how Hippo and Potto gave Mouse a taste of his own medicine.
Did you enjoy it?
Mouse didn't!